# RANNOSAURUS

## By
## Nick Ward

*little bee* 🐝

# Many, many years ago...

when the world was a wild and dangerous place...

... when everywhere was covered with volcanoes and jungles...

... and when fierce dinosaurs ruled the earth...

...the

fiercest

dinosaur

*Carythosaurus*

*Apotasaurus*

*Iguanadon*

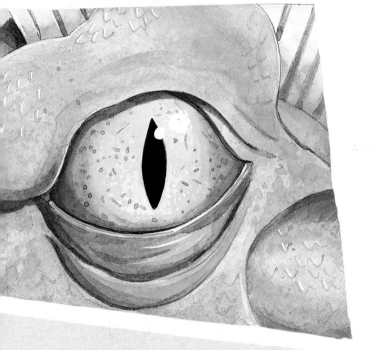

# of all was...

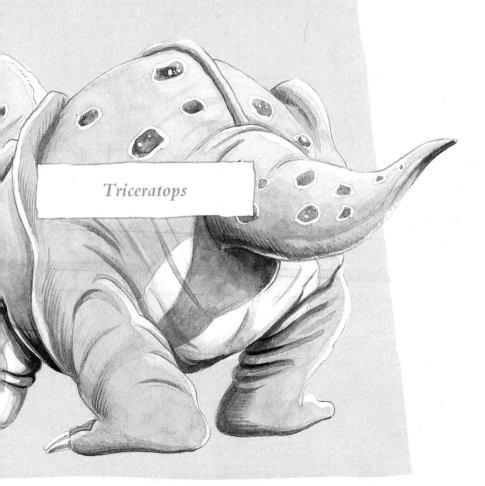

*Triceratops*

...Tinyrannosaurus
(wrecks).

Because he wasn't as big as some of the other dinosaurs, Tiny had to be especially fierce to make up for it.

So he had learned to roar the loudest roar...

ROAR!

SLAM!

... clash his jaws the hardest...

... and pull the fiercest faces.

He was the loudest, hardest, fiercest and grumpiest little dinosaur ever!

Even as a baby,
Tiny had been a handful.

He stamped and
growled and would
kick up a storm.

**But today...**

...Tiny was even grumpier than normal.
He had an awful toothache,
which was not good news,
as everyone knows dinosaurs
love to **EAT!**

Dino
Pops
Tasty bits
of gravel

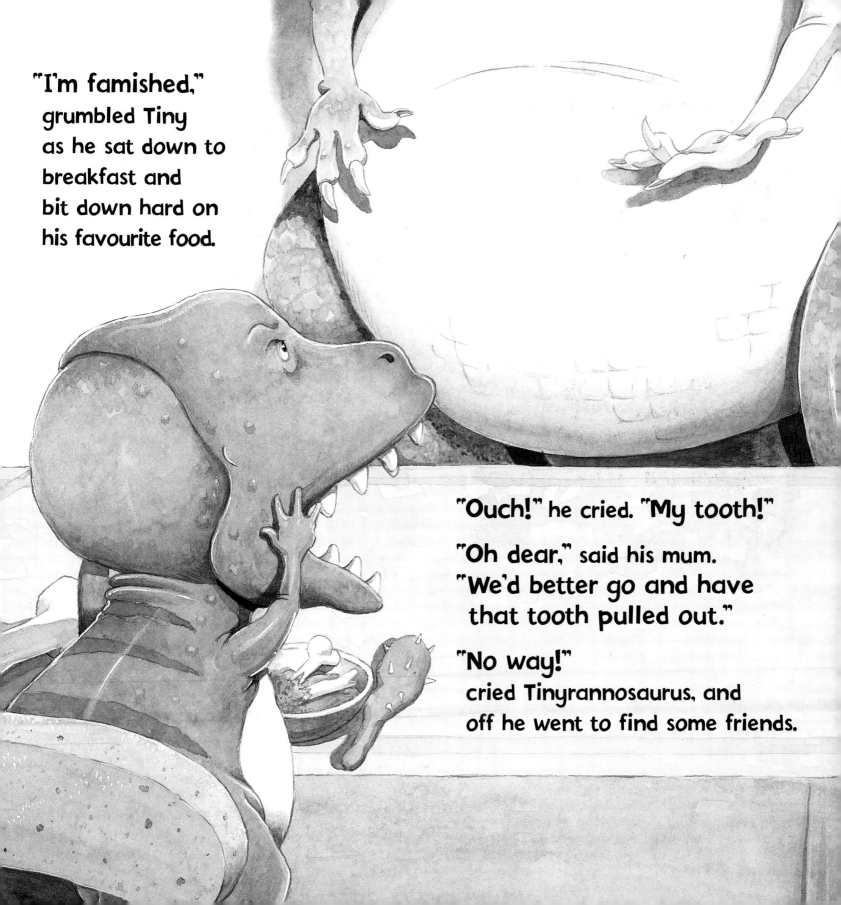

"I'm famished,"
grumbled Tiny
as he sat down to
breakfast and
bit down hard on
his favourite food.

"Ouch!" he cried. "My tooth!"

"Oh dear," said his mum.
"We'd better go and have
    that tooth pulled out."

"No way!"
cried Tinyrannosaurus, and
off he went to find some friends.

Tiny stomped through the jungle
in a grumpy mood. His tooth ached
and his tummy was empty.

Then, just around the corner,
he came upon Triceratops
eating in a clearing.

"**Food!**" smiled Tiny.
He roared his loudest roar.
He pulled his fiercest face
and bellowed...

*Charge!*

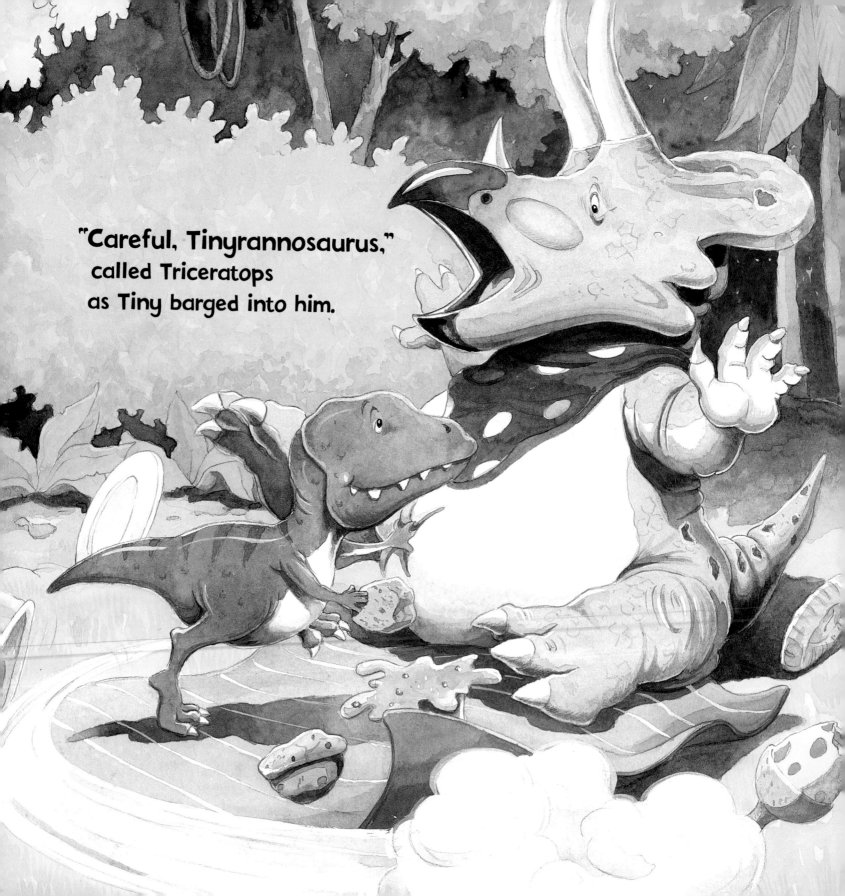

"Careful, Tinyrannosaurus,"
called Triceratops
as Tiny barged into him.

Tiny stomped down to the river.

"I'm starving," he moaned,
and then he smelt fresh berries...

... and followed the scent
to a group of Apatosauruses.

"Charge!"
he yelled
and stormed
towards them...

... picking up
a huge bunch of berries
and slamming shut
his mighty jaws.

"Ow! ow! Ouch!"
he cried. "My tooth!"

"Oh dear," said the Apatosaurus.
"Perhaps you should see about
having it removed."

"I won't have it removed!"
sobbed Tiny and stomped off
up the nearest volcano...

Food!

...where he found
his best friend Vilo C Raptor
who was eating an apple.

**"YeoOoowwwwwouch!"**
howled Tiny.

"What's the matter with you?"
munched Vilo.

"I'm sorry, Vilo," said Tiny,
"But I'm so hungry, and I've
got a terrible toothache."

"Then perhaps
you'd better go
and have it
taken out,"
said Vilo.

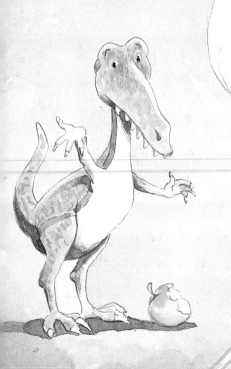

**"NO!"** screamed Tiny

**"I WON'T HAVE IT REMOVED!"**

... and stamping and roaring
and growling and grimacing...

... Tinyrannosaurus kicked up
a **REAL STORM,**
until the clouds churned
and lightning flashed everywhere.

But when the dust settled, Tiny still had a terrible toothache and an empty tummy.

"Oh dear," he sighed. "Perhaps I had better have it removed."

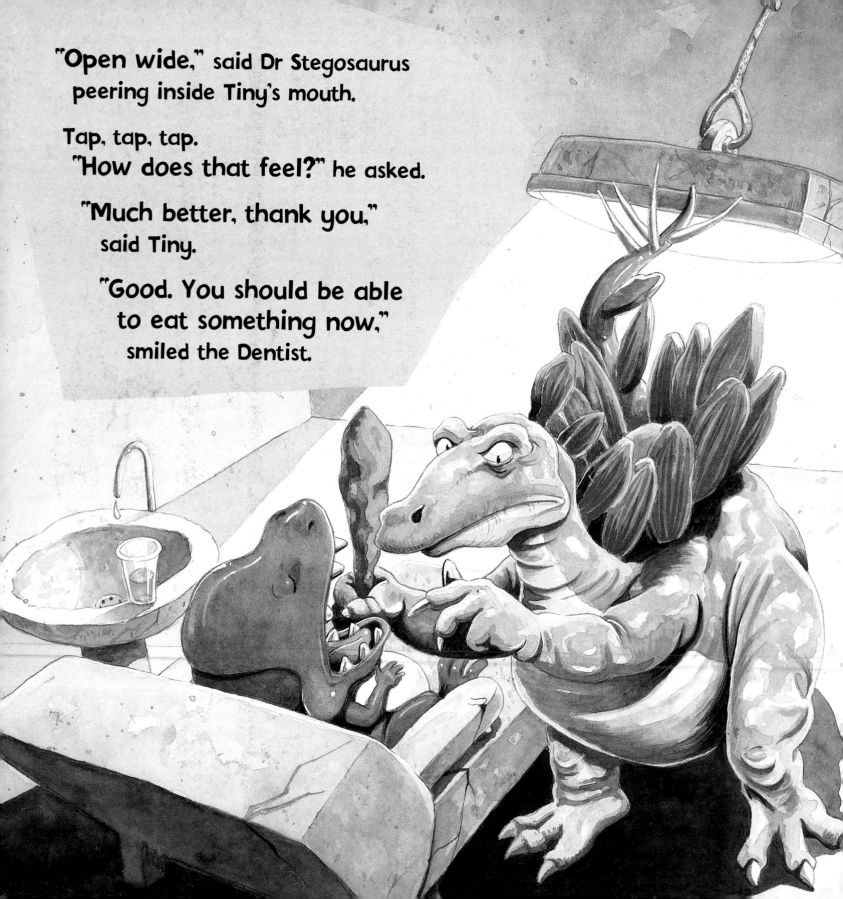

"Open wide," said Dr Stegosaurus peering inside Tiny's mouth.

Tap, tap, tap.
"How does that feel?" he asked.

"Much better, thank you," said Tiny.

"Good. You should be able to eat something now," smiled the Dentist.

"I can?!" said Tiny, and jumped up, mouth open, and went

CHOMP!

# For Mickybrockosaurus,

from one old dinosaur to another!

## N.W.

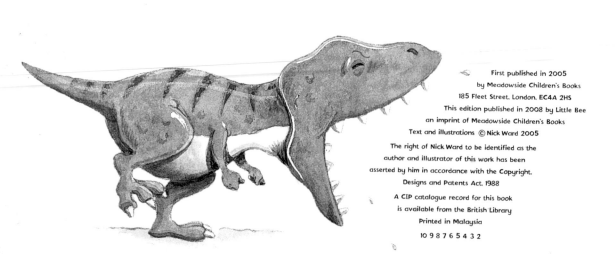

First published in 2005
by Meadowside Children's Books
185 Fleet Street, London, EC4A 2HS
This edition published in 2008 by Little Bee
an imprint of Meadowside Children's Books
Text and illustrations © Nick Ward 2005

The right of Nick Ward to be identified as the
author and illustrator of this work has been
asserted by him in accordance with the Copyright,
Designs and Patents Act, 1988

A CIP catalogue record for this book
is available from the British Library
Printed in Malaysia
10 9 8 7 6 5 4 3 2